E
Moo

We Are Adopted

Text: **Jennifer Moore-Mallinos** / Illustrations: **Rosa M. Curto**

BARRON'S

We Are Adopted

I'm so excited! Today I'm going with Grandma and Grandpa to the airport to pick up my new baby brother. I can't wait to meet him and I can't wait to be a big sister!

When I was adopted, Mom and Dad took a plane to Russia to pick me up and bring me home. The only difference is that I was born in Krasnoyarsk and my brother was born in Volgograd.

When we arrived at the airport, Grandma and Grandpa took me to the gift shop so I could pick out a special gift for Mikhail. Mikhail is Russian for Michael. Even though Mikhail is only six months old I think he is going to love the blue fuzzy bear I picked out just for him.

It seemed like we were waiting forever, then finally we saw Mom and Dad come through the doors. Mom was carrying the baby and Dad was carrying the suitcases. As soon as they saw me they smiled and hurried over to where I was standing with Grandma and Grandpa. They must have really missed me 'cause Dad picked me up and gave me the biggest bear hug ever and Mom gave me a big wet kiss on my forehead! Then Mom introduced me to my new baby brother, Mikhail.

Mikhail's so cute! He has brown hair and brown eyes, just like I do! When I gave Mikhail the blue bear that I picked out for him, he smiled and cooed at me. Then Mom handed me a present and said that it was from Mikhail. Mom said that if Mikhail could talk he would say that he wanted to give me a special gift for being his big sister! I couldn't believe my eyes when I saw the Russian dolls Mikhail gave me! Each doll fits inside another, they are called *Matrioshkas*, and all the kids in Russia have them!

On the way home from the airport, Mom and Dad told us of all the things they saw in Russia and that one day they were going to take me and Mikhail back to Russia so we can see where we were born. Even though we are now growing up in a different country, Mom and Dad want us both to learn about Russia and its culture.

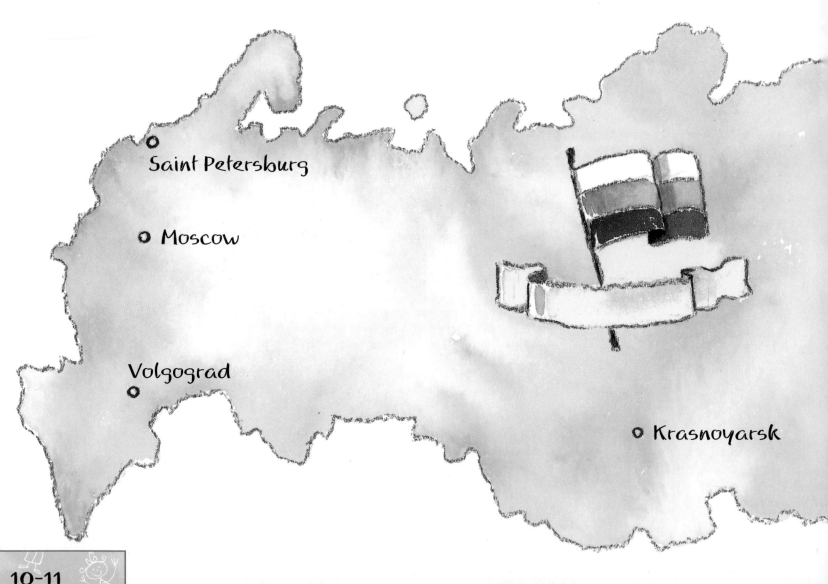

Saint Petersburg

Moscow

Volgograd

Krasnoyarsk

- Gah-loob-TSEE •

- KRAH-bah-vee sah-LAHT •

- sehl-YOD-kah pad SHOO-boy •
("Herring under a fur coat")

Ingredients:
4 thick, salty herrings
5 potatoes
4 carrots
4 beets
5 eggs
14 oz mayonnaise

- sah-LAHT oh-lee-VYEH •

Ingredients:
5 potatoes
3 carrots
4 eggs
1 lb chicken
7 oz peas
3 dill pickles
salt
9 oz mayonnaise

Ever since I was very little, Mom and Dad have been teaching me about Russia. Mom likes to cook Russian food once a week and Dad's always bringing home books about Russia for us to read. I can sing the alphabet in Russian and Mikhail loves it when I sing songs to him in Russian too!

Learning about Russian culture and the cultures of other lands is a lot of fun. Mom and Dad have been taking me to a special picnic where we learn about many different cultures, including Russian. All the kids at the picnic have been adopted from many different places around the world, just like me and Mikhail. Some of the kids were born in Korea and China and some were born in Africa. Some of the kids were even born in this country.

The picnic is decorated with flags from all around the
world and there are different kinds of food from each
country for us to taste! Kids from each country take turns
playing their music and showing off their special dances.
Last year we learned a traditional dance from China.

Every year there are games and races for the kids and even a magic show. While the kids are busy having fun, the parents talk to each other about being parents. Mom and Dad's best friends started coming to the picnic last year after they adopted Jessie from Korea. I can't wait to take Mikhail to the picnic this year too!

When I was old enough to understand, Mom and Dad told me that I was adopted. At first I thought that being adopted meant that I was sick or that there was something wrong with me, but then Mom and Dad explained to me what being adopted meant. When Mikhail gets older, Mom and Dad will explain it to him too.

When I was born, my Russian mother was unable to take care of me, but, because she loved me very much, she hoped that another family would take me with them. When Mom and Dad saw my picture and read the story of my short life, they decided to adopt me!

They told me how happy they were when they found out that we were going to become a family…Mom said that the hole in their hearts was suddenly filled with love and that I was the greatest gift they could ever want!

I might not have Mom's blue eyes or Dad's long legs but I'm smart at math like Mom and I'm good at building things like Dad. Although our Russian mothers were different, Mikhail is now my brother and I am his sister and Mom and Dad are our parents. We're a family no matter what!

Being a family is about loving
and taking care of each other and
that's what we do! And just like
other families, some things upset
us. Mom drives me crazy when
she keeps reminding me to make
my bed and Dad's singing hurts
my ears. Mikhail is too little and
too cute to drive anybody crazy,
but maybe when he gets older
he will too!

I'm glad
to be me!

28-29

Treasure Book / Family Album

Everybody loves a family album! It's a story of your family; a time sequence of events. More than once you have opened a photo album with family and friends to take a trip down memory lane. How you've all changed! Time seems to fly, and very quickly.

A family album is so much more than just a book of pictures! It's a book of treasures with past experiences and fond memories. There's a story for every picture.

Creating a book of treasures is a great way for parents to tell the story of their child's adoption. Your child will be able to follow along through the adventure of how you became a family while enjoying all the pictures and other items you choose to put in your book.

A treasure book is personal, individualized to your own family. It's your very own story!

Items to use in your treasure book may include:

- plane tickets to and from your child's country of origin
- pictures of your child's country of origin
- mementos from the orphanage or child care facility
- baby pictures
- hand prints
- a flag from your child's home country and a flag from your country
- birth certificate
- welcome home pictures and extended family.

Be creative with other ideas!

To get started you will need a photo album or scrapbook, glue, scissors, stickers, markers, crayons, glitter glue (optional) and imagination! Since your treasure book is a story of how your family came to be, you might want to start at the beginning and proceed in chronological order.

Have fun!

Recipe Box / Book

What a great idea! Giving your child a taste of his or her homeland is a great way for the whole family to experience culture firsthand. Not only will your child love to taste some culinary delights, but so will you! Of course, first you need to find some recipes!

Gathering recipes from around the world is so easy now. Good resources include the Internet, your public library, travel agencies, and even the adoption agency.

To make your very own collection of recipes you will need a shoebox or scrapbook, recipe cards or lined paper, art supplies including scissors, glue, markers, crayons, stickers, and glitter glue. Maximize participation and ask your child for help decorating the box. According to his or her age, your child may provide suggestions, indicate preferences, and perhaps even help with some manual work. As you gather recipes, add them to your recipe box/book. After you have tried each recipe, you may want to rank each one according to its success with everyone.

Enjoy!

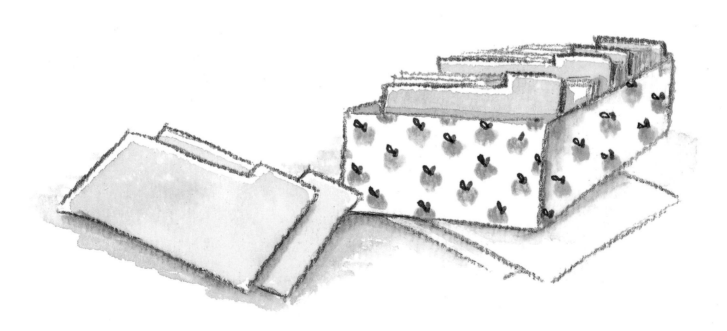

Frame of Fame

We would all love to see ourselves in a picture frame decorated with items that represent who we are. Just as the photo captures a special moment and tells a story, so can the surrounding frame.

To make your very own Frame of Fame, you can either use a store-bought wooden frame or a frame made out of cardboard.

To make a frame out of cardboard, simply cut a desired size and shape out of a piece of cardboard (1). Note the folds that must be made to the sides so that the frame can stand upright. Then cut out the center, as shown by the dotted lines. Decorate the front with items of your choice. Tape the chosen photo to the back of the cardboard frame (2) or use another piece of cardboard as a backing.

If you use a wooden frame, glue items of your choice around the outside of the frame. Be creative! For example, if you are using a photo of you and your child arriving home from your child's country of origin, you might decorate your frame with flags from both countries.

Using a larger frame with many spots for pictures can be a great way to present your family story. Once the frame is finished, move the vertical folds back (3) and the frame will stand by itself (4).

Be creative!

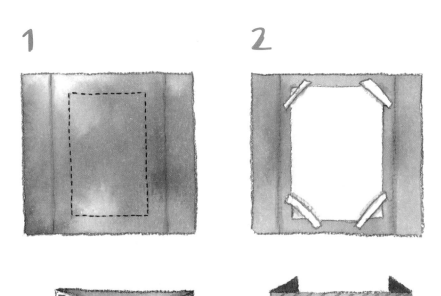

C hildren of all ages from all around the world are in need of loving homes. Fortunately, through the process of adoption, many of these children will be successful in finding a family able to provide love and support.

Adoption

As many of you know, the road to adoption can take several months and even years. As a result, prospective parents may experience many emotional highs and lows during their journey through the adoption process. Although this emotional roller coaster can be stressful and time-consuming, the gift of a child certainly makes the journey well worth the ride.

Deciding to adopt a child is a very big decision and not one that can be taken lightly. There are many things to consider, particularly if the child's place of origin is different from your own.

For many prospective parents, the overwhelming desire to have a child will often supersede any concerns regarding the child's origin, color, race, and ethnicity. Although these factors may not be of great importance at the time of adoption, it is something that will eventually need to be addressed with your child.

Physical concerns

There are many concerns adoptive parents share regarding their child's physical and emotional health. Frequently, when children are adopted from another country, some of their health-related issues are not apparent at the time of adoption. Common ailments usually associated with a child's stay in an orphanage or care facility include malnutrition, respiratory infections, and digestive and skin problems. After a relatively short time in their adoptive homes, most of these children will show a remarkable change in overall health. Within the first year following adoption and with appropriate medical treatment, most children show significant improvement.

Emotional concerns

The emotional condition of a child will vary depending on both the age of the child and the circumstances of his or her previous life. For example, a child's ability to bond with the adoptive parents will occur quite easily and at a faster pace when the child is an infant. On the other hand, older children may be less sure of their new surroundings. As a result, they may need more time to develop a sense of trust. Patience is required for children who are emotionally fragile.

Sleeping difficulties such as falling asleep and nightmares are also experienced by many children following their arrival to their adoptive home. With patience and reassurance, your child will eventually overcome sleeping anxieties, and going to bed will no longer be such a difficult event.

Talking about adoption to a child

Many adoptive parents choose to inform their child at a very early age that he or she is adopted. Experts agree that adopted children should also be told about their birth origin.

Although children may feel loved and wanted by their adoptive parents, they may still be curious about their birth parents, their place of origin, and the circumstances that led to being adopted. Parental reactions vary when these questions begin. Some parents may feel threatened and find it difficult to support their child's need to satisfy this curiosity; others see it as an opportunity to help their child to learn more about his or her birth country and its culture. Recognizing that your child sees and loves you as a true parent may make it easier for you to understand that it is quite natural for a child to want to explore his or her background. If your child also asks questions about birth parents and if you have information that is appropriate to share, it is best to provide this according to the child's readiness. When children are ready to explore these issues, they will do so at their own pace.

It's also important to keep the explanation short and simple. There are many wonderful books for children about adoption that both you and your child will enjoy. Your child will be quite impressed with all the efforts you made to make him or her such an important member of your family!

Adopting a child is an incredible experience. It's an opportunity to share your hearts and home with a child in need of a family. Many lives are touched by the presence of a child, especially one you have chosen to be your very own.

As children are settling into their new homes, they may appear apathetic. For example, eye contact may be limited, and facial expressions such as smiling may be infrequent. Some children will engage in rocking behavior as a way to calm their anxiety. This kind of behavior can be attributed to overexposure to sensory stimuli that sometimes occurs after a child's stay in an orphanage or care facility. It is therefore suggested that stimulation be introduced in a controlled and gradual way. In a calm, predictable atmosphere, your child will soon be able to process many of the feelings and emotions he or she is experiencing for the first time.

WE ARE ADOPTED

First edition for the United States and Canada
published in 2007 by Barron's Educational
Series, Inc.
© Copyright 2007 by Gemser Publications S.L.
El Castell, 38; Teià (08329) Barcelona, Spain
(World Rights)
Title of the original in Spanish: *Somos adoptados*

Text: Jennifer Moore-Mallinos
Illustrations: Rosa M. Curto

All inquiries should be addressed to:
Barron's Educational Series, Inc.
250 Wireless Boulevard
Hauppauge, NY 11788
http://www.barronseduc.com

ISBN-13: 978-0-7641-3787-7
ISBN-10: 0-7641-3787-5
Library of Congress Control Number 2006938824

Printed in China
9 8 7 6 5 4 3 2 1